THE LITTLE HELP

Paula Helps Prevent Air Pollution

D1589052

Claire Culliford   Illustrated by **Emma Allen**

Paula is a parrot. She's a squawky-talky parrot.

Paula loves the sound of her own voice. As she's young, she's only just discovering the different noises she can make.

Paula is an adventurous parrot. She loves flying through the trees in the rainforest from branch to branch.

Her mother always tells her to be careful and not to go too far.

Paula and her friends like to fly around
and make lots of noise when visitors
come to see them in the forest.

The visitors take photos of them with their cameras
- CLICK-CLICK-CLICK. It's almost like the parrots are film stars!

Unfortunately, some days Paula has a cough.
Her best friend Priya often has a cough at the same
time. On these days, their mothers don't let them go out
to play. So they stay at home and rest their voices.

Paula and Priya don't understand why they keep coughing.
It seems to happen when there are lots of visitors in the forest.

One day, Paula is at home. Her mother has given her some berries to help her throat and told her to rest her voice, and her wings.

"Mum, my throat hurts again," says Paula, in between coughs.

"I know, dear. But if you rest your voice today then tomorrow you'll feel much better," says her mum. She gives Paula's back a gentle stroke with her wing.

"But why does the cough keep coming back?" asks Paula, a little scared. "Is it something serious?"

"Oh no," says her mum. "The cough you have is because of the cars that come to the forest. Some of them have bad engines that produce fumes which make the air dirty. That causes air pollution."

"The fumes get stuck in your throat if you get too near to them. You young parrots like to fly around close to the visitors. So the fumes get into your beaks."

"Do all cars make me cough?" Paula asks.

"There are some cars with good engines," Paula's mum explains. "Those cars don't make fumes at all. They're better for your throat and for the air too. They're even better for the trees in the forest!"

When she's feeling better, Paula rushes to tell
Priya what she's learned from her mum.

"What do you think we should do?" asks Priya. "I like flying
around the visitors, but I don't want to keep getting a cough."

Paula, who is an adventurous parrot, can't bear the thought
of not being able to fly around. So she starts to think. And
then, she has an idea. "Perhaps we could just fly around the
visitors that come on a bicycle or on foot?" she suggests.

"That's a really good idea," says Priya. "Maybe we could
fly around the visitors that come in cars with good
engines too. We'll just avoid the visitors who come in
the cars with bad engines that make fumes."

"Perfect!"
squawks Paula.

And so, once they are better, Paula and Priya put on a display for the visitors again – flying up, down, all around, and screeching and squawking at the top of their voices. However, they make sure to avoid visitors who come in the cars that make bad fumes.

This probably leaves some visitors very confused. They have been told you can always see parrots in this forest. Yet some visitors don't see any parrots at all!

As the visitors realise over time what is happening,
more and more of them arrive in cars with good
engines, or on bicycles, or even on foot.

Paula and Priya notice that their coughs have stopped, so they can
fly around the visitors again. Everyone is happier! The visitors
get to see the parrots - CLICK-CLICK-CLICK - and Paula and
Priya have helped make the air in their forest much cleaner!

Questions for discussion

Does air pollution make the air dirty or clean?

What kind of cars have good engines?

Can you find out what the car fumes
from bad car engines are made of?

University of Buckingham Press, 51 Gower Street, London, WC1E 6HJ
info@unibuckinghampress.com | www.unibuckinghampress.com

Text and Illustrations © Claire Culliford, 2019, 2021
Illustrations by Emma Allen, 2019

The right of the above author and illustrator to be identified as the author and illustrator of this work has been asserted in accordance with the Copyright, Designs and Patents Act 1988. British Library Cataloguing in Publication Data available.

Print: 978-1-80031-644-7
Ebook: 978-1-80031-645-4

Set in Kabouter. Printing managed by Jellyfish Solutions Ltd
Cover design and layout by Rachel Lawston, lawstondesign.com